UNBRIDLED
PASSION

THE FAB FOUR

UNBRIDLED PASSION

by Ros Asquith

ORCHARD BOOKS

ORCHARD BOOKS
96 Leonard Street, London EC2A 4RH
Orchard Books Australia
14 Mars Road, Lane Cove, NSW 2066
ISBN 1 86039 444 2 (hardback)
ISBN 1 86039 635 6 (paperback)
First published in Great Britain 1998
First paperback publication 1999
Text and illustrations © Ros Asquith 1998
The right of Ros Asquith to be identified as the author of
this work has been asserted by her in accordance with the
Copyright, Designs and Patents Act, 1988.
A CIP catalogue record for this book is available from the
British Library.
Printed in Great Britain

☆ CHAPTER ONE ☆

"Oh, I wish you could understand how much I love you," Flash blinked back a tear as she hugged her favourite pony. Flame was a chestnut gelding, just 12 hands high, with a roman nose, stubby legs and a very shaggy mane indeed. He looked more like a baby guinea pig than a pony and more like a cuddly toy than either. Flame was due to be retired from the riding stables that month and Flash was sure he would go to the knackers to be made into pet food. Flash had asked if she could look after Flame but the riding instructior just laughed like a drain and said, "In a council flat?" He added it

was nothing to do with him – it was up to the owner who was never there. Flash had worked every spare hour at the stables to earn money to save Flame. She had worked out exactly what to do. She already had £60 and was planning to ask the stable owner about it that Sunday. But she hadn't told anyone yet, not even the Fab Four.

"I love you so, so much," she continued, stroking Flame's funny little crooked white blaze, "but no one wants you any more, you're too old, you're just too old."

"I'm not that old," said a cheery voice in her ear. Flash squeaked. Her dream had come true!

Flame could talk!

"Not that much older than you, I should think," the voice went on.

Flash blushed scarlet. It was hard to say which was redder, her face, her hair, or Flame's forelock. The voice, naturally, was not a pony's voice. Even if ponies could speak (and Flash was sure that with the right training and a lot of kindness they could) they would be likely to have a sort of whinnying, snuffling tone. This voice was certainly a boy's voice. A rather soft, American drawl. And there was only one voice that Flash knew that sounded anything like that, and that was Tom's. Tom was the gorgeous new stable boy who everyone fancied and Flash, though she didn't like to admit it, could see why. She could see why especially at this moment, as she turned, her face the colour of a London bus, to look at him. He had blond hair and the kind of California surfer's tan that you don't get on a wet English October afternoon. His green eyes twinkled mischievously at Flash as she turned to face him.

"I m-meant Flame was old," stammered Flash, thinking that if the ground opened now and she disappeared forever it might be worth it, just to have bathed in that smile.

"That's all right then," gleamed Tom. "You coming up tomorrow?"

"Oh... yeah," said Flash trying to be casual. She nonchalantly patted Flame's neck. Then she rather less nonchalantly disentangled her watch strap from his mane before sauntering out of the yard and tripping gracefully over a bucket.

"Whoopsy," said Tom, helping her up with a strong arm and beaming another rocket powered grin that made Flash dizzy.

She was late for a meeting of the Fab Four and rang them to suggest they start without her. She was definitely feeling a teensy bit, well, wobbly.

☆ CHAPTER TWO ☆

"That's not like Flash," said Lizzy, putting the phone down and sounding distinctly put out. "We've been waiting for ages. Still, we can fill her in when she gets here. It's not that important. We only want to talk about fancy dress, after all."

The Four were meeting to discuss their costumes for the community centre Halloween party, which they had been going to every year since they were seven years old.

"B-but it's r-really s-special this y-year," murmured Owl. "Cos th-they're giving a big prize to the best costume. C-cash."

"How much?" The others were excited. Usually all the winner of the under sixteens got was a bag of nuts and oranges.

"N-not sure. B-but quite j-juicy," said Owl.

"Juicier than a bag of oranges?" laughed Lizzy.

"I am definitely going as a ghosty," declared Eclaire.

"Oh boring," scoffed Lizzy "There'll be zillions of ghosties."

"But none as big as me," continued Eclaire. "I want to be covered from head to toe. I'm not risking being laughed at like last year..."

Lizzy remembered that Eclaire's poisonous mushroom costume last year had got a rather unkind response. The stem had looked a little lumpy, as it had been made for someone about a quarter of Eclaire's size.

"Fair enough, but couldn't

we go as something a little bit different?" said Lizzy.

"Like what?" snorted Eclaire.

"Well, um. How about vampire bats? Or werewolves? Or giants?"

"Ahem," muttered Owl. Height was a sore point with her.

"You could be a small giant," said Lizzy.

"I think w-we should go as the Three Witches," said Owl. "You know – 'B-bubble, b-bubble, t-toil and trouble.'"

"You're obsessed with Shakespeare. Not everyone knows that stuff," said Eclaire. "Anyway, there'll be even more witches than ghosties and there are supposed to be four of us."

Just at that moment, the bell rang.

"Well, there might be four of us now, if Flash has bothered to turn up," said Lizzy grumpily, swooping out to open the front door.

"I'm really sorry," panted Flash. "Something came up at the stables."

"Oh, 'something came up' did it?" Lizzy asked

crossly, "*something* more important than the Fab Four?" She thought Flash looked a bit odd.

Flash blushed. She had been thinking about Tom all the way to the meeting. She was sure it showed, she didn't know how to cover it up.

"What's up, Flash?" said Eclaire, the minute she came in.

Flash blurted out the first thing that came into her head.

"W-well, I was going to tell you before, but I thought you'd think I was stupid," she started.

Immediately, all the others looked sympathetic.

"We n-never th-think one of the Fab Four is s-stupid," said Owl. "Remember our chant."

And all of them solemnly chanted:

"All for one and one for all
Fatty, skinny, short and tall
Frizzy, Flash, Owl and Eclaire
Stick together, foul or fair.

Four for one and one for four
Funny, clever, rich and poor

Frizzy, Flash, Eclaire and Owl
Stick together, fair or foul."

"OK Flash, spill the ketchup," drawled Eclaire in a fake American accent. She always said 'ketchup' instead of 'beans' and it had always irritated Flash. It especially irritated her now, when a real American accent was on her mind, but she did her best not to let on. She did not feel like admitting her brand new crush on Tom, just yet.

"I'm worried that they're going to murder Flame," she blurted out.

"Murder? Murder WHO?" shouted the others all together.

Flash explained Flame was a pony. They calmed down, but only a little bit.

"See, he's old and I heard the stable owner saying he was going to be retired next month and you know what that means."

"Not really," said Lizzy.

"It means he'll be sent to slaughter. For pet food. Or he might be sent to France, to be eaten by people."

"Yeuk," spluttered Eclaire.

"Loads of countries eat horses, not just France," said Flash, who had read a lot about the subject. "In fact, we ate tons of horse meat over here after the war."

"Urg. You mean our Mums and Dads ate it?"

"Well... probably. Or our grandads, anyway."

"Well, I don't see how it's so different from eating any other animal," said Lizzy firmly.

"Lizzy! How could you? This is a pony that Flash loves! It's like eating a pet!" said Eclaire. "I mean, you wouldn't eat Snuffles, would you? Or Owl's goldfish?"

"Mmmmmm. For a teeny snackette between meals. Followed by a little roasted kitten with gerbil sauce," Lizzy laughed.

She was stopped by a stifled sob from Flash.

"But I love him!"

"Who?" asked Lizzy sharply. She felt there was

more to Flash's mood than a pony, however important a pony might be.

"Flame of course," said Eclaire, immediately rushing to Flash's side with a big hanky and a bigger hug.

Lizzy felt very mean and guilty.

"Well, obviously we must save him," she said. "How much money have you raised?"

When Flash told them, they could hardly believe their ears. It seemed like an absolute fortune.

"But that's far more than we helped to raise for your Mum's birthday shoes!" said Eclaire.

"I know," mumbled Flash, "That's why I didn't tell you. I didn't want you all to go through that again. But it costs about £10 a week to keep a pony in a field, you know, for hay, worming, foot clipping and stuff. Then there's the rent of the field, too. Plus I'll have to pay the stables what they would have got from the knacker, which is about £40... so what I reckoned was to get a month's money plus £40, which is £80, and then I can make the rest as I go along..."

The others were amazed at Flash's organisation.

"B-but aren't th-there ch-charities?" asked Owl.

"Yeah. But they don't take any old pony jus' cos someone's fond of it. They'd be swamped," Flash replied.

Lizzy took charge. "Flash, I really wish you'd told us before. This is much more important than a Fancy Dress party. I'll find out about Horse and Pony Charities. Eclaire can help ring round and maybe Owl, you could find out if your dad knows any farmers who have a field spare?"

"Brilliant," said Owl, whose father worked in a place that made agricultural machinery.

They all agreed to meet again in two days' time, to discuss how far they'd got.

"We can put the finishing touches on our Fancy dress, too," said Eclaire.

"Oh, um, yeah," murmured Flash, whose mind was drifting towards a pair of green eyes and a dazzling smile. She tried to think of Flame, but Tom's image kept getting in the way.

☆ CHAPTER THREE ☆

Flash raced to the stables the next day straight after school, but Tom wasn't there. Desolate, she did her usual mucking out and polishing of tack and was crying into Flame's mane when she felt a hand on her shoulder.

"What's up?" said a tender voice.

"N-nothing," sniffed Flash, then she realised Tom might think she was crying about him, which was partly true. So she added "It's just Flame. He's being retired next week and I'm worried he might go to the knacker's."

"Oh, how cute! You don't want to cry about

that," Tom chuckled, "he's sure to be put out to grass, dear l'il ol' pony like that."

"Do you really think so?" sniffed Flash.

"Sure," Tom went on, "Hey... your hair looks amazing against his mane! Like two baby foxes."

My HAIR? Amazing?

Flash was speechless. Her hair? Amazing? She'd never given it a thought before, unlike Lizzy, who was always worrying about her frizz. She just washed it and tossed it. In fact, Flash never gave her appearance any thought at all. But here was the boy-of-her-dreams paying her a compliment. She suddenly wished she'd thought about it a little bit more – and bothered to remove the boiled egg from her shirt front before coming...

"Course, it could do with a brush," smiled Tom. And then, seeing Flash's downcast look, he added kindly "You know 'brush' that's what you call a fox's tail, isn't it?"

"Oh, yeah..." Flash shuffled, desperately casting around for something to say. She just couldn't think of a quick witty reply.

"So you think Flame's sweet?" was all she could manage.

"Sure is," murmured Tom, adding, "you too."

To Flash, the silence that followed this remark seemed endless. In fact, it was only a couple of seconds before Tom was cheerfully slapping Flame on the haunch and saying, "Well, night-night, I gotta lock up early tonight."

Flash's heart plummeted into her plimsolls. She had thought of nothing but Tom for twenty-four whole hours. Was she only going to see him for five minutes?

He flashed her a six zillion megawatt smile,: "You are coming back tomorrow night aren't you? To clean the tack? You will come, won't you?

No one else will be here to help."

"Oh, sure, no trouble," said Flash, realising that her voice was around four decibels higher than usual. She tried to lower it, "See you tomorrow then," she growled, swiftly tugging her watch strap from Flame's mane and making the poor pony squeak. Flash carefully walked around the bucket on her way out of the yard and turned to give Tom a casual wave, stepping backwards, as she did so, into a small pile of manure.

"Oh, that's good luck you know," she boomed.

"Your throat OK? I got some great throat pastilles," shouted Tom.

"No, fine," trilled Flash. She scampered off as though a bit of horse dung on a plimsoll was all she needed to make her full of the joys of spring.

☆ CHAPTER FOUR ☆

"You will come, won't you? No one else will be here to help..."

Tom's words rang in her ears. Could this be love? But why hadn't she taken up his offer of a throat pastille? It would have given her a few more minutes with him...

That night, Lizzy rang.

"Flash! Great news! Owl thinks she knows a farmer who'll put Flame in his field. He's only going to ask for feed money, because he's happy to have Flame there as company for his own pony! Isn't that amazing?"

"Oh. Great," said Flash, guiltily. She wasn't sure how to tell Lizzy that she had other things on her mind now, bigger, more important things than ponies. Anyway, she knew now that Flame would be all right. Tom had said so.

"Well, you certainly don't sound that thrilled," said Lizzy crossly.

"I am," said Flash quickly. "It's just that, um... well, why didn't Owl ring me herself?"

"She's been trying all evening," said Lizzy. "But you've been out. Where have you been?"

"I'm allowed out, aren't I?" snapped Flash. "I've been at the stables, anyway, seeing Flame," she added guiltily.

"Oh. That's all right then. Sorry I asked. I thought you'd be pleased," said Lizzy huffily.

"Oh, I am," said Flash. "Look, we can talk about it at the meeting, OK? I've got to dash." And she put the phone down, feeling bad, but also feeling she never had a moment to herself, there was always someone wanting to know what she was doing. Surely she had a right to some privacy? She really needed some time to just think... about Tom.

Lizzy was not happy after her conversation with Flash. She went next door and rang Eclaire's bell.

"What's up?" mumbled Eclaire, who came to the door in a vast cook's apron decorated with a small flowery pattern and large floury patches.

"Gotta talk," muttered Lizzy, stomping upstairs. "Can I come in?" she shouted over her shoulder, as an afterthought.

Eclaire disappeared into the kitchen before following Lizzy up to her bedroom.

Lizzy had slumped down on one of Eclaire's enormous fat soft cushions, sulking. She brightened up at the sight of Eclaire, who was carrying a trayful of meringues and cream and two glasses of passion fruit popsicle, a queen among drinks.

"So? Spill the ketchup," said Eclaire.

"I'm fed up with Flash. First, she can think of nothing but saving a pony – then, she loses interest."

"What do you mean?" asked Eclaire.

"I just told her about Owl and the field and she sounded like she couldn't care less," said Lizzy, furiously kicking a bean bag.

"Oh calm down," soothed Eclaire "She was probably just in a hurry or something. Wait till the meeting, I bet she'll be over the moon."

"I hope you're right," stormed Lizzy. She hated arguing with any of the Fab Four and although it hadn't exactly been an argument she'd had with Flash, she still felt very peculiar about it. But no one in the world was as soothing as Eclaire. The combination of Eclaire, meringues, big fat cushions and passion fruit popsicle soon made Lizzy feel she'd made a mistake and there was nothing wrong with Flash after all.

That night, Flash dreamt of Flame, but he was

being ridden, in a cowboy saddle and bridle, by Tom. Tom wore a Stetson, long leather boots, and was whirling a lasso in Flash's direction. Flash was just thinking how nice it might be to be caught by the lasso when Flame started bucking like a bronco and Flash woke up in a sweat.

Then she remembered what Tom had said: "You will come, won't you? There will be no one else here to help."

But there was a Fab Four meeting! She couldn't cancel it, Lizzy would be furious. And yet, and yet... To her surprise, Flash realised that she wasn't torn at all. She wanted to see Tom much, much more than she wanted to go to the Fab Four meeting. She suddenly felt grown up, in love, free.

But when Lizzy collared her in the playground she wasn't so sure.

"Owl's going to bring all the details about the field, what it will cost and everything," said Lizzy.

"Look, it doesn't matter any more," blurted Flash. "Flame's not going to the knacker's. It's all OK."

"That's great," said Lizzy "How come?"

"I just know, that's all," Flash paused, and then said, "Tom told me, you know, the stable boy."

"Oh," said Lizzy, feeling rather flat. "Well, that's great. Now we can concentrate on getting gear for the Halloween do. See you later."

"Yeah, fine" mumbled Flash, feeling guilty. If she went straight to the stables after school, maybe she could make a date with Tom and then get to the Fab Four meeting just a little bit late. Yes, that's what she would do.

Flash sped to the stables on her bicycle and swerved into the yard hoping against hope that Tom would be there early too.

Throwing down her rusty old bike, she flung open the tack-room door and there he was, polishing a saddle. He glanced up, lighting the murky room with a radiant smile.

"Fantastic. It's just so great you're here," he said.

Flash's heart skipped a beat. The combination of the speed of her bike ride, the romantic gloom of the tack room, the gleam of Tom's eyes, the flop of his floppy blond hair and the fact that he was so clearly pleased to see her all made her breathless. She tottered slightly and grasped at a bridle overhead to steady herself. The bridle and a halter swooped off the hook and miraculously wound themselves round most of Flash.

"Whoopsy," said Tom, gliding out of the gloom to help remove the browband, which was threatening to strangle the already hyperventilating Flash.

Flash was just thinking how much she loved the way he said 'whoopsy', when she realised that somebody else was there

She turned to see a girl teetering in the doorway.

"Oh... Hi Cindy," and Tom turned the full glow of his gleaming grin in a wide arc away from Flash and towards the figure in the doorway.

Cindy had the kind of long blonde hair you never see in real life, only on dolls. Her eyes, which were several sizes too large, were forget-me-not blue. The extreme shortness of her mini-skirt made her legs look even longer than they were already. For a second Flash wondered if she was on stilts. She was, in fact, wearing very high

stilettos, but Flash hardly had time to take any of this in before she heard Tom say: "This is Flash, she's helping me clean the saddles."

"Oh, how sweet," simpered Cindy. "And she doesn't mind smelling of horse plops and saddle soap?" She accompanied this devastating wit with a high, tinkling laugh and added, "Do you always wear a bridle on your head?"

"Oh, she loves horses," said Tom, "and it's great she's here to finish, cos now we won't be late for the movie."

"Oh, lovely," giggled Cindy and before Flash could say a word, she saw Tom wave cheerily and leave arm in arm with Cindy.

"See you tomorrow, kid," he beamed.

Kid. Kid! KID! Flash spluttered and fumed. Why, he

was only a year or so older than her himself! What was he doing with that older girl? It was disgusting, it was horrible, it was... Flash yanked at the bit, which was still round her shoulder, threw the bridle on the floor, overturned the saddle and stormed out in a rage. That was it! Tom would get the blame for the unfinished work, not her!

Blinking back tears, Flash cycled off, determined to go to the Fab Four meeting as though nothing had happened. But on her way, as her anger cooled, she knew she had to do something to make Tom notice her. She was sure, that if Cindy hadn't come in just then, something would have happened. She had felt that Tom might be about to kiss her, and although she hadn't been sure she wanted that, she still felt, well, cheated. Cheated of the chance to kiss. Or at least to say 'no'.

Did he really just see her as a kid? A foxy, horsy girl? Someone with no glamour? She was going to have to change.

☆ CHAPTER FIVE ☆

Eclaire, Owl and Lizzy were all sitting stony-faced when Flash arrived. The meeting was at Owl's so they were all squashed under the tiny platform bed and the only space for Flash to sit was on the floor.

"What's up? Someone died?" Flash attempted to joke.

"You're late," said Lizzy angrily, staring at the tiny scrap of floor not occupied by Flash.

"Only ten minutes!" snorted Flash. "What is this anyway? A teacher's group?"

Eclaire was hurt by her sarcasm. "Flash, it's a

bit much you know, we've all been running around in circles trying to work out ways to help you save Flame, and now Lizzy says there's no need. And you swan in as if you never cared in the first place."

"What do you mean? What have you all done?" asked Flash, with a sinking feeling.

"Lizzy and I rang up all the charities and got them to send leaflets," continued Eclaire.

"Y-yes," added Owl, with unusual vigour, "And m-my dad r-rang about f-fifty f-farmers."

"Yeah. And I even rang two slaughterhouses to see what happens to the ponies. And that wasn't much fun," added Lizzy.

There was a long silence. Flash felt that if she could disappear in a puff of smoke it might be better for everybody.

"Anyway, are y-you s-sure F-Flame is going to be all right?" Owl asked kindly, knowing Flash needed a bit of help to speak.

Flash breathed a sigh of relief.

"Yes, I'm quite sure. Tom said he'd be put out

to grass. He said he was a 'sweet l'il ol' pony' – so it must be true."

Something about the way Flash said these words, combined with the fact that she was blushing, alerted Lizzy.

"Flash, you don't fancy this Tom do you?"

"No!" Flash said hotly. She looked round at her three friends. She could see instantly they didn't believe her.

"No!" the disbelieving silence continued. "Well, I did. A bit. I suppose I still do. Only..." Flash felt, to her horror, that she was about to cry.

"Only what, Flash?" Owl asked in her tiny, kind voice.

"Only – he's got a girl friend and... and I just wish I was tall and blonde and wore high heels and mini-dresses and it's all horrible," admitted Flash.

The others gathered round to comfort.

"Poor Flash why didn't you tell us?" asked Eclaire.

"I've only just found out," said Flash. Then,

☆ 35 ☆

with some of her old never-say-die spirit returning she declared: "I'm gonna change myself! I'm gonna look like her! But better!"

"Oh Flash! Don't be so daft! You look lovely as you are," said Eclaire.

"Look I understand about wanting to look nice, but you don't want to look like some girly off Page Three," snorted Lizzy.

"I-I th-think it m-might be quite fun, s-sort of d-disguising yourself," said Owl, kindly. Although it wasn't just kindness. Her passion for acting meant she loved the idea of dressing up.

"Yes! Why shouldn't I?" said Flash. "I'm sure if you could all see him, you'd understand. You know, he has this floppy green hair and blond eyes and..."

Flash mixing up her words led to such gales of laughter that even Flash cheered up.

"Green hair's reminded me of our main mission," said Eclaire when they had all recovered. "What are we going to wear for Halloween?"

They decided to spend Saturday morning at the market getting face paint, masks and anything black or green. The party was Saturday evening, so they could spend the rest of the day kitting themselves out.

"Yeah. It'll help you forget about Tom," said Lizzy, meaningfully.

"OK," said Flash, with a heavy heart.

When Flash got home, the not-very-nice, not-very-clean lodger Snake was lurking about.

"You still upset about that pony?" he sneered.

☆ 37 ☆

"No," Flash felt furious. She did everything she could to avoid Snake. Why was he here, in her old room, anyway? If only her mum could afford not to have a lodger... She stumped off to have a bath.

In the bath, Flash day-dreamed. She saw herself, transformed into a leggy blonde, sauntering into the stable yard. She saw Tom look up, enraptured.

"Flash, is that you? Y-you've changed," he gasped, before sweeping her into his arms. No.

That didn't feel quite right. She replayed the scene. "Flash. You look wonderful. Can you ever forgive me for last night? Cindy's my sister. I just got her to do that to make you jealous. Will you come out with me tonight? Please say you will..."

No. She liked that one, but she had to admit it wasn't likely.

Perhaps she would arrive and find him in tears, because Cindy had chucked him. Then she could comfort him...

Or maybe she would arrive to find him with Cindy. That would be dreadful. But he might see her over Cindy's shoulder and realise that Flash was much more beautiful and that he'd made a terrible mistake...

By now, the bath water was stone cold and Flash could hear her mother banging on the door.

"Come on sweetheart, you'll catch a cold. Come and have a muffin."

And she dragged herself out to sit cosily by the gas fire with her mum and to wonder which of her daydreams would come true.

☆ CHAPTER SIX ☆

On Saturday morning, Lizzy was relieved to see Flash there bright and early. They all trawled up and down the market place, looking for ghoulish make-up. The stalls were stuffed with pumpkins, fangs, witch hats, broomsticks, but Lizzy was determined to go as Frankenstein and wanted to find a really convincing joke bolt to wear through her neck.

Flash saw her chance.

"Let's go to Horrids department store. They've got loads of brilliant jokes there," she said.

"Y-yes. And I might find a t-troll wig," said Owl.

"A troll!" laughed Eclaire. "I thought you were going as a baby giant."

"M-most amusing," huffed Owl, as they all trooped off to Horrids.

Eclaire and Lizzy headed straight to the fifth floor in search of toys and jokes and Flash said she'd help Owl find a troll wig.

In the wig department, Flash confided in Owl, "Please don't tell the others," she hissed, "but I am going to dress up for Tom. Just once. It can't do any harm. Can it? Will you help?"

"OK," said Owl, doubtfully.

Owl quickly realised she was rather excited at the idea. She had always wanted to try on really expensive wigs. She and Flash chose the longest blondest ones they could and nipped into a changing room to try them on. The results were not quite what they hoped. Owl was drowned in cascades of wig and looked like a shetland pony trying to be a racehorse; Flash's face looked a completely different colour under the golden wig – she became a washed out salmon pink.

"Hmmmm..." said Flash gloomily. "He did say my hair was nice, like a fox."

"Why n-not t-try a red w-wig then?" suggested Owl, busily trying on a mass of troll-like curls.

Flash thought she looked very flash indeed in the red wig, but when she took it to the till, she nearly fainted.

"It'll cost me nearly all I've saved!" she gasped.

"You mean a wig could cost as much as a real live pony?" gasped Owl. "There must be much more hair on a pony."

"Not the same quality of hair, madam," said the sales assistant, snootily.

"Er, do you h-have ch-cheaper, sort of party-type wigs?" whispered Owl shyly.

"Fifth floor, novelties," the assistant turned away and hurried towards a more likely looking client in shades and a designer suit.

Flash and Owl trudged up to join the others and Owl found a brilliant green and purple wig which seemed to be made of wire wool.

"Let's go to the shoe bit," said Flash.

"What do you want shoes for?" said Lizzy suspiciously.

"I've decided to go as the Bride of Dracula," said Flash, quick as a flash and winking at Owl. "And I reckon red stilettos are what I need."

The others were impressed and they all enjoyed trying on the shoes and tottering about.

"Do people actually wear these for fun?" Eclaire giggled.

"I believe so, madam." Another frosty assistant caused Flash to wonder whether they cloned these women in some secret laboratory and then sent them out into the world to frighten customers.

"Psssst," she whispered to Owl. "Maybe we should dress up as Horrids assistants for the party."

She unfortunately chose the moment when Owl was balancing on the very highest pair of heels that were small enough to fit her tiny feet. She was wondering whether this was the solution to being knee high to a flea when Flash's remark made her explode with mirth. She fell right over onto a rather gorgeous autumnal shoe display which was decorated with real leaves and twigs, sprayed gold and silver.

The clones from the secret laboratory surged towards Owl in a throng making clicking noises.

"Help," thought Flash "They'll make her pay for it."

"Whoopsy" said one of the assistants, sending a shiver through Flash. But although this had sent her thoughts flooding to Tom, she was relieved to see that the assistants were actually quite human. They were all more worried about little Owl than the display.

"Where's your Mummy then?" they asked kindly.

Poor old Owl, thought Flash. She was so small, everyone was always trying to look after her, even horrible Horrids clones.

Flash bravely marched up to the till with the shoes she had set her heart on, only to find out that they had been put in the half price sale section by mistake. The magnificent scarlet leather shoes cost nearly as much as the wig! She would just have to find some second hand stuff. Or second foot.

The girls ended up buying vermilion lipstick, thick black false eyelashes and green powder for

Flash, and green and white face paint for Lizzy and Eclaire.

On the way out, Flash bought a very cheap swathe of sparkly material. "I can wrap this round me like a mini-dress," she whispered to Owl. And then she said loudly, "This is just the kind of lurid thing Dracula's bride would wear, isn't it?"

"Right. Back to my place to dress up," said Eclaire. And off they marched.

The Fab Four all spent a long time experimenting with make-up.

"You've got to get me looking, you know, pretty," said Flash as Eclaire tried vainly to stick the false eyelashes on for her. "I'll do the scary bits, like drips of blood coming out of my nose, just before the party."

Eclaire did her best, painting on eyeliner and lipstick, until Flash was satisfied.

Then, while Lizzy and Eclaire were experimenting with bolts, sheets and fake scars covered in scabs, Flash whispered to Owl, "Look, let's go over to your sister and see if she's got any fancy shoes."

"W-we're just going to my place," said Owl to the others. "To get some Troll stuff. Back in half an hour," and off they went.

Owl's big sister Loretta was highly amused when she heard the girls' plan. But when she heard what they wanted, she nearly died laughing.

"Stiletto heels! What d'you think this is... 1952?"

"But that's how his girlfriend dresses," explained Flash.

"All the more reason to look different," winked Loretta "She won't last five minutes if you look coooooooool."

"What is cooool then?" asked Flash, feeling desperate.

"Cooooooooool is hi-tech trainers, girl. Loads of money. Cooool is black tights, black top, an' more eyeliner than you've ever seen."

"So you don't reckon on this, then?" asked Flash sadly. She opened her coat to reveal her scarlet spangled swathe, which she'd wrapped round herself rather lumpily.

"No offence darling, but you look like something the postman wouldn't forward," hooted Loretta. Then, feeling she'd been a bit harsh, she told the girls they could rummage around in her wardrobe.

"Thanks Loretta! I wish I had a sister like you!" said Flash, flinging her arms round her.

"You wouldn't if you had t-to l-live with her," mumbled Owl.

The girls started to rifle through Loretta's clothes.

"She's got more clothes than the Queen," whistled Flash.

"She th-thinks she is the Queen," Owl said grumpily. "Anyway, I th-think her ideas are r-really boring. It'd b-be m-much more fun to dress up l-like you were going to. Like a film star." Owl looked wistfully at Flash. She loved the idea of dressing her up as a film star from an old Hollywood movie. Owl had in mind a low cut lime green dress... black patent shoes, a little patent bag... a circlet of diamonds. It was not a look she could ever imagine achieving for herself.

But Flash was feeling confused. She'd spent her whole life as far as she could remember, in checked shirts and jeans. That was what she was comfortable with. Cindy's look was one thing and Loretta's look was another. But what should her own look be? Who was she, anyway?

Flash ended up borrowing a pair of black tights and a tunic and Loretta's trainers. The trainers were three sizes too big, but easier to walk in than the high heels at Horrids had been. She didn't have the heart to go back to meet the others with Owl, it would have been too difficult to sneak off again.

"Tell them I'll see them at the party," said Flash, "I've got to go and wash my hair."

Owl sloped off mournfully, wishing she'd never tried to help Flash. It hadn't worked out and she felt worried about Flash's feelings for Tom. They seemed to her a bit unreal. After all, she hardly knew him.

☆ CHAPTER SEVEN ☆

Flash cycled home and washed her hair four times, trying to style it in different ways. Each time it looked less and less like a fox. She was relieved her mother was out, since she did not want to run into anyone while she was wearing the false eyelashes.

She dressed up, arranged the tunic sixteen different ways, wound a scarf round her neck, then round her hair, then round her waist, then tossed casually over her shoulders. She decided it looked best round her waist. She felt pretty pleased with herself by the end. The eyeliner and lashes certainly made her look dramatic and, she thought, about four years older, like Cindy. But the trainers, she had to admit, were a joke. Her feet just swam about in them and she felt like she was wearing two paddle steamers.

Feeling very excited and extremely naughty, she decided she would blow her money on the latest pair of incredibly expensive, dazzlingly coool trainers. She knew they cost nearly as much as the wig, but why not? She'd earnt it after all and she'd spent her whole life worrying about money. Why not have some fun, instead? She zoomed off to the sports shop. Yes! They had a pair of Ghetto-vipers just her size. Well, they were one size too big, but it didn't matter because they looked absolutely wonderful and they had a purple flash down the side! This, she convinced herself, was a Good Omen.

They were ten pounds more than she thought. If she bought them, she would be cleaned out. But Flash was so obsessed with Tom, she bought them anyway.

Her 'look' was now complete.

Last-minute addition of cheapo fake fur coat pinched from mother

She took a bus to the stables. She wasn't about to risk a flat tyre or scuffed trainers on the way. She thought the bus conductor was giving her rather a strange look, but she was too busy rehearsing her speech to Tom to take much notice.

In Flash's head, the conversation went something like this:

Tom (with an admiring look): Flash, you look fantastic.

Flash (carelessly): I guess I've just grown up a little, Tom.

Tom: You sure have (this remark is accompanied by a long slow whistle).

There is an awkward pause, in which Tom blushes.

Flash: I've only got ten minutes, so I'll clean one saddle and then fly.

Tom (crestfallen): That's really sad – I was kinda hoping you...

Flash (through lowered lashes in a silky voice): Yes? What were you hoping?

Tom: That, that you and me might, you know,

hang out? Maybe take in a movie later?

Flash: No way. I'm meeting someone else. Got a party. (Pause) Maybe tomorrow.

Tom (ecstatic): Hey, that would be great.

This daydream caused Flash to miss her stop. Luckily the rain was only falling lightly when she got off, but the track to the stables had turned into a mud pit. Flash was carefully picking her way through, trying to tread only on the dry bits to preserve her dazzling trainers when she was startled by a strange squeaking noise. It sounded like the noise Flame had made when she pulled her watch strap out of his mane. But much louder. Then she heard a voice like Tom's only much sharper.

"Hey, calm down. Crazy nag!"

Hang on a minute, that was Tom's voice? And now the whinnying sounded really frightened and she was sure she heard a slap! What was happening? Wishing she had brought her bike, Flash broke into a run. Her stupid, mega-fashionable trainers were as useful for running as a pair of stilettos. They were too high and too big and she twisted her ankle, skidding and landing in a swampy ditch to the side of the track. Covered in mud, she pulled herself up, tore off her trainers and rushed, as fast as her swelling ankle would allow, through the driving rain towards the horrible noise.

As she turned the corner she saw a big horse van. She was just in time to see a glint of chestnut flank before Tom closed the ramp and waved the driver off.

What was happening? Was Flame going out to grass already? And no one had told her?

"No! That's Flame! Stop! Stop! I want to say goodbye!" Flash panted. But the noise of the van revving up drowned her voice. She could hear Flame whinnying inside as the van swept past, the driver either not seeing, or ignoring her as she flapped her arms wildly. Another great swoosh of mud was churned up by the wheels and, to add insult to injury, splattered all over the now drenched Flash. Blinking hard, she ran after the van. Oh No! What was that written on the side? No! No! It read:

N. Acker & Sons Ltd Suppliers of Meat Products to the gentry.

Flash limped after the van, shouting and weeping, but it turned into the main road, gathered speed and swept away. In despair, she turned back and trudged up to the yard. She must tell Tom. He would know what to do. He'd obviously put Flame in the wrong van. Or maybe, a ray of hope dawned, maybe there was a chance that this van was just being used for ordinary work, just taking ponies to vets, or fields, or something. Yes, that must be it, surely. Flash hoped against hope.

Flash blundered into the tack room, which was even more gloomy than usual. Tom was calmly polishing a saddle.

"Hi, Flash. Didn't think you'd make it in this rain."

"Tom! Tom! Don't you realise what that was? You just put Flame in a knacker's van!"

"So?" Tom was looking at her in mild amusement. The only clean bit of her face were where her tears had left two sparkling white trails. Suddenly he leapt back, looking nervous. "Ugh! Is that a tarantula?"

Through her horror and dismay, Flash realised that one of her false eyelashes had peeled off and was now roosting on her cheek. Not that it mattered. Nothing mattered except Flame.

"Didn't you hear what I said?" she shouted. "I said that was the knacker's van! And Flame was in it!"

Flash knew that as soon as Tom realised what had happened, he would be horrified. He must have thought that the van was from the vet's or a charity.

"Oh, I thought it was the RSPCA," he laughed.

"Tom! It's not a laughing matter! We've got to ring the knacker's straight away and tell them there's been a mistake…"

"Oh, come on, he's only an old Spanish kebab pony. Plenty more where he came from," joshed Tom, adding "I thought you were coming to help, but you're obviously off to a Halloween do."

Flash burst into tears. Obviously, she did not look glamorous, not after her run through the mud and rain. But had Tom really said what she thought he'd said? 'A Spanish Kebab pony?' He *knew*, then. There hadn't been a mistake. Tom knew all along that Flame was going to be slaughtered. But he didn't care. He hadn't even cared enough to tell her the truth, so she could have done something. Flash had heard the phrase "Idols have feet of clay" before. It meant that nobody was perfect and you should never imagine they were. For a long slow moment, the phrase danced about in her mind. Her idol, Tom, lay in shattered fragments.

Tom suddenly looked uncomfortable, "Hey, come on Flash. There are lots of healthy young ponies to be looked after. And at the end of a useful life why not make more use of a pony? The slaughterers are kind enough people, they do the deed quickly and cleanly. It's stupid to care so much about one pony."

Flash just stared at him in disbelief.

"Look, I can see you really care, and I'm sorry that I let you think he was going out to grass. Besides it's Saturday today, they won't bump him off till Monday," Tom went on trying to be kind.

"Bump him off? Bump him off! You have no SOUL!" screamed Flash and disappeared, limping, into the twilight.

Flash's spirits at this moment were lower than they had ever been. What, she wondered, had happened to her? She had been obsessed with Tom. She had believed him too easily. What had he actually said about Flame? That he was going out to grass? That he was a 'sweet l'il ole pony'? Maybe he had only said he was *probably* going out to grass... and when did being 'sweet' protect a horse from the knacker's? She remembered reading something about it once, called 'Bye Little Pony' about a girl whose pet was blind or something and had to be put down. Flash had to admit she was so smitten by Tom that she had just stopped caring so much about Flame. Or her friends. But now she cared terribly. By far the worst thing was, that although there might still have been time to save Flame, she now had no money to do so. She had spent almost all her cash on some crazy, stupid, crippling, mud-splattered, horrible, loathsome trainers – that were now lost forever in some muddy ditch. How could she have been so stupid? How? How? How?

But there was a tiny ray of hope. Although Flash felt she had abandoned her friends, she knew that they would always rally round in a crisis. Maybe they could think of some way to make up the cash. She would have to phone them anyway, to say where she was. She stumbled through the drizzle to a phone box, with her soaked socks squelching at every painful step. And a sorry sight she looked, her hair plastered over her face and her remaining false eyelash perched on her nose. Her tights and tunic were ripped and covered in mud and blood from the brambles that had torn at her arms during her mad dash to the stables.

She used her bus fare to ring Lizzy, then Eclaire, then Owl. No one was at home. Desolate, she began to walk back through the rain.

☆ CHAPTER EIGHT ☆

Lizzy, Eclaire and Owl had got fed up with waiting for Flash.

"Sh-she said she was j-just going to wash her hair," said Owl, although Owl was feeling quite worried. Could Flash have gone off to see Tom before the party after all? Owl had thought she was going tomorrow. She didn't feel she could tell the others that Flash had been buying clothes as much to dress up for Tom as for Halloween although of course even Owl didn't know about the trainers.

"Well, I think we'd better go round to hers.

Maybe she's drowned in the bath or something," said Eclaire.

"Why should we bother?" said Lizzy fiercely "she's not bothered much about us, recently."

"All for one and one for all," chanted Eclaire, making Lizzy feel mean and ashamed.

"It's supposed to work both ways though," she huffed, and dragged herself off Eclaire's cosy cushions. "OK let's go. But if she's not there we'll just go to the party without her."

The three girls, who'd made themselves look like three ghouls, filed out. Lizzy looked spectacular,: she had covered herself in green face paint and had adapted a real metal bolt and taped it to her neck. This was somewhat heavy and caused her to lurch along with her head on one side rather like the hunchback of Notre Dame.

Owl had covered her face in purple, pink and lime green spots to match her wig. She had fangs and a bathrobe with bits of old rubbish stuck to it.

Eclaire, in her enormous sheet, made a rather friendly looking ghost. That was Eclaire for you, thought Lizzy. She just didn't have an unkind bone in her body.

When they got to Flash's block of flats, Owl insisted they walk up the stairs.

"I am n-n-n-not going t-to take a l-lift to the thirteenth f-floor. N-not on Halloween!" she declared as firmly as her fangs, stutter, and tiny voice would allow. In fact, the three girls were glad of each other's company, as the night was now full of bangs, wails and ghostly noises. Pumpkins flickered from all the windows and the atmosphere was spooky.

They rang Flash's bell.

The not-very-nice-lodger Snake opened the door, gasped and immediately slammed it shut again.

"It's the awful Snake," the three ghouls murmured. "He probably doesn't know it's Halloween and thinks we're loonies."

They banged again. "It's only us!"

Snake re-opened the door, smirking.

"Where's Flash?" asked Lizzy.

"Gone down the stables," grunted Snake.

"Oh no!" The girls realised Flash must have been really serious about Tom, to have missed the Halloween Party.

"Oh no," whispered Owl to herself "I th- thought she was going down tomorrow."

"She's lost her marbles then," muttered Lizzy, feeling she had been right all along. "Unless it's something to do with Flame?"

Just at that moment, Flash's phone rang and Snake went to answer it, leaving the door open.

"Nah. Your mum's gone to a party," said Snake. "Your mates have just turned up, though."

It must be Flash! Trying to get her mother!

Eclaire rushed in and pulled the phone from Snake's hand "Gimme that... *Please*!" she added as an afterthought.

"Flash! It's me, Eclaire. Where are you? What's up? Oh no! When? How much? Oh no!... Flash? Flash?"

Eclaire banged the phone and shouted some more, then hung up.

She turned to others. "It's all terrible," she wailed and told them all she had heard. "Flash spent her money – *on a pair of trainers* – and now Flame is going to be slaughtered and we can't save him!"

Eclaire turned to Snake.

"Where's Flash's mum?"

"Gone to a party," sneered Snake.

"What will we do?" moaned Eclaire.

"We'll get the money," said Lizzy firmly. She felt a kind of relief, somehow, that they had something to do. She was also glad to know that Tom had been shown up. She had had a bad feeling about it all along.

Owl felt the worst of them all. She had to do something. But what?

"E-even if we get the money," said Owl, "w-we m-may not be able to save him if he's gone off in a van already."

"We'll cross that bridge when we come to it. We'll go to the knacker's yard and plead. We've just got to get it," said Eclaire.

"How much?" said Owl

"I'm afraid it must be the price of those trainers – and you know how much that is," said Eclaire, feeling quite angry for the first time "what a waste!"

"T-to th-think, we could save a pony's life with that money," murmured Owl, thinking of the expensive wigs she and Flash had tried on and feeling slightly sick.

"You mean that pony is really going to die?" asked Snake.

"Yes. What do you think we're talking about?" said Lizzy rudely.

"Stop arguing and think," Eclaire commanded.

They thought and thought some more.

Eclaire thought, if only she had a couple of

meringues and a nice big dollop of cream, it would help her think more clearly.

Lizzy thought, if only she had told Flash what she really believed about Tom, maybe they wouldn't have got into this mess.

Owl thought, if only she hadn't encouraged Flash to dress up, Flame would still be all right. This wasn't true, of course, because if Flash hadn't gone to meet Tom, she would never have found out that Flame was going to the knacker's. But just at that moment, every one of the Fab Four was busy blaming themselves.

"I know!" said Lizzy suddenly "Let's get money trick-or-treating! We can bang on people's doors and say we're trying to save an old pony and people could give us money instead of sweets?"

"And squirt silly string through their letter boxes if they don't," laughed Eclaire. "I can't see how we can get enough, but at least it's better than doing nothing."

"B-but p-people n-never give m-money unless

it's a ch-charity," Owl complained.

"It is a charity!" Lizzy was impatient. "It's to save a pony! We'll make people believe us," and she and Eclaire swept Owl along with them. Just as the three ghouls were opening the door, they heard a voice.

"Would this help?" They turned in irritation at the sound of Snake's whine. But he was holding out a ten pound note. "I like ponies," he said rather sadly.

"Oh, thanks, thanks a lot," said Eclaire, ashamed of herself.

"Wow, Snake. Thanks really really much," they all said. They galloped down the stairs, thinking they had been so mean to Snake, but he was really quite kind. They couldn't wait to tell Flash.

☆ CHAPTER NINE ☆

They decided the only way to raise a lot of money quickly was to go to a different house each.

"But don't go in, whatever the person says," warned Eclaire "And only stay really close to each other and do houses that are next door to each other."

"Yes ma!" said Lizzy.

Hopefully, they approached three friendly looking homes with nice gleaming pumpkins in the windows.

"If you're collecting money, you should have a card from a charity," said the woman who opened the door to Lizzy. "But you can have a tangerine."

Owl's door was opened by a witch who looked so terrifying that Owl fled.

Eclaire got a very cross man who said he wished he'd never let his kids put a pumpkin in the window. He'd been bothered all night and why didn't she clear off?

They got similar responses in the next twenty houses they visited: nobody gave them money and all they got was three bags of sweets, four apples and six tangerines.

"I give up," puffed Eclaire, who had demolished most of the sweets and fruit single-mouthedly.

"Yeah. Whose stupid idea was this?" groaned Lizzy.

"Oh, no," said Owl, who had just had a thought. A big thought. A very, very big thought. A very big thought indeed.

"What is it Owl?" asked sympathetic Eclaire, who was always keen to help.

Owl slumped down on a low wall. "Y-you know where we should be? We should be at th-the party. We should be trying to win the fancy dress prize."

The full gloom of the situation suddenly struck both Eclaire and Lizzy at once. They had thrown away their real chance of getting money by trailing round houses "Oh, how could we have been so stupid?" raged Lizzy. She kicked the wall in frustration. "Ouch! I've broken my toe!" she had kicked the wall much harder than she had meant to and was now leaping about squealing.

"Don't be such a drama queen Frankenstein," said Eclaire, unusually sharply. "We've got to go like the wind."

"We'll have missed it by now," moaned Lizzy, gazing anxiously at her foot and wiggling it from side to side. It felt better already but she didn't like to admit it. "I just can't believe we did this! How could we have been so daft? We didn't think. We just did the first thing that popped into our heads."

"The first thing that popped into your head," Eclaire felt like saying. But she was too kind, and let it go. Instead, she said, "If we run all the way there, we might just be in time. They're not announcing the winner till 9.30."

So saying, Eclaire gathered her voluminous luminous sheet around her, and galumphed off into the night. Lizzy made as much as she could of her limp, but her long legs had no trouble keeping pace with Eclaire's little squashy ones. Owl's teensy stumps had to whir like a propeller for her to keep up with the others. Owl's wig fluttered. Lizzy's bolt bumped. Eclaire's sheet flapped. Passers-by applauded the ghoulish trio as they zoomed through the dark streets, skidding to a halt outside the welcoming green glow of the Community Centre.

"You've missed all the fun," hissed a vampire at the door.

But one glance inside the hall told Lizzy they still had a chance. She could see all the entrants lined up on stage, and the judge was only just climbing up onto the stage to inspect them. The judge was the local mayor, a very small woman in a very pink suit. As the girls watched, the mayor started to walk very slowly down the lines of spooks, talking to each one as though she was the Queen visiting an orphanage.

"Quick," whispered Lizzy. "Let's nip up on the end of the row." And the three scuttled through the audience, which was made up of proud parents and an assortment of small spiders, witches, ghosts and bats too shy to enter, and clambered on stage.

All the competitors were bathed in a ghostly green light, and Owl felt that if she hadn't been sandwiched between Eclaire and Lizzy, she might have felt a tiny bit frightened. As it was, she felt a strange, almost overpowering feeling of excitement. "I'm on a real stage," she thought to herself, "with a real audience. This is how it must feel to act. Scary, but wonderful at the same time." She gazed around her. She was so small all she could see were legs, and a pretty peculiar lot of legs they were, too. There were knobbly green ones, furry grey ones, skinny orange ones and a few pairs with hooves, or claws. She suddenly felt very stupid in her cheap wig and spotty make-up.

Lizzy was feeling much the same. Oh! If only she'd spent some money on that Frankenstein mask at Horrids instead of doing it all herself! The judge was taking ages and Lizzy could feel sweat trickling under her bolt, which felt heavier and heavier until it seemed like a ball and chain.

Eclaire was now regretting her decision to dress as a ghost. Sure, she wouldn't get laughed at, but she wouldn't get noticed, either. There were about twenty identical looking sheets standing on stage and several more shy sheets in the audience. The only thing that outnumbered ghosties was witches. It would have been better to risk being laughed at to get noticed. Why hadn't she come as a pumpkin? She was exactly the right shape and there was only one of those...

But now, the judge was approaching...

"And what is your name?"

"Eclaire... I mean, Claire", said Eclaire, reddening under her sheet.

"Lovely," smirked the judge. "I hope your mother won't miss her bed clothes."

"And what a dear little fairy," she said, turning to Owl.

"She's a troll!" hissed Lizzy.

"Of course. Lovely. And how old are you?" asked the judge, patting Owl's wig in an irritating manner.

"Good heavens! Really?" laughed the judge, as Owl stuttered her age. The judge turned to Lizzy.

"Aha! And here we have..."

"Frankenstein," said Lizzy, miserably.

"No, dear, Frankenstein was the man who invented you. YOU are Frankenstein's monster."

"Erp," gulped Lizzy. What was this? School?

"Still, it's a lovely bolt," crooned the judge, gliding back down the line.

"We haven't got a hope," muttered Lizzy.

Finally, the judge strolled to the front of the stage, tapped the microphone and announced:

"This has been the most impressive display. It makes one proud of one's community to have so many boys and girls willing to work hard and deck themselves out in such splendour for us... Even if some of them have just borrowed their parents' bed linen. Ho ho ho."

She droned on like this for what, to Lizzy, Owl and Eclaire, seemed like hours.

"I'm starving," whispered Eclaire. "Why doesn't she just get on with it?"

"Shhh!" hissed Lizzy. "She's announcing the winners."

"Third prize," boomed the Judge, "which is a lovely pen and pencil set donated by Mrs Blanket, goes to the gorgeous little troll outfit." And she beckoned to Owl.

Owl blinked in amazement and tottered forward to cheers.

In her imagination, she was taking a bow in a West End theatre – having singlehandedly been the first woman to play all of Shakespeare's leading men.

"Speak up, dear," shouted the judge, as she tried to catch Owl's name. But Owl didn't care.

She could work on her voice some other time. Suddenly she was sure, absolutely certain, that Lizzy and Eclaire would win second and first prizes. And so were they. They were so sure in fact, that they edged forward in anticipation and when the judge said "And second prize goes to the magnificent Frankenstein's monster..." Lizzy zoomed to the front of the stage. She held her large green paws aloft and made clanking grunts in the hopes of scaring the shy ghosts and tiny bats gazing up admiringly at her from the audience. She could feel all the other competitors slapping her on the back and she could hear them cheering her on. It was only when she got to the very front of the stage that she realised that the hands that she had thought were patting her on the back were in fact trying to hold her back. And the voices cheering her on were in fact jeering. The awful reason for this was obvious as she reached the judge's side. A much greener, hairier and altogether meaner and scarier monster was also lumbering towards the judge. This, monster was the winner of the second prize. It had a big bullet head and a much better bolt. Lizzy sloped back to Eclaire's side, blushing furiously beneath her face paint. She tried to ignore the loud cackles of laughter coming from the little ghosts and bats and witches.

"And now, the first prize, the very generous sum of £30 donated by," and the judge announced the name of a leading stationers, although everyone was too impressed by the amount to listen... With money like that Flame could be saved, no doubt about it. "This marvellous prize goes to the excellent Zombie!" and she gestured to a lanky figure in black, caked in layers of mud and very lifelike looking blood.

"Oh no!" Eclaire felt like crying. Their chance of saving Flame had gone now, forever. She gazed in admiration at the Zombie, who drew shrieks of terror from the little ghouls in the front row. It had been a brilliant idea to roll in real mud, the creature really did look as though it had stepped straight from a grave.

"Thank you, thank you," screeched the Zombie, flinging its mud spattered arms round the shrinking judge.

"Aaaaargh!" shrieked Lizzy in amazement, dashing forward at the sound of the Zombie's voice. "It's Flash!"

After much rejoicing and crying and back-patting and hugging, the Fab Four agreed to meet at seven o'clock the next morning. They would take the train to the slaughterhouse and beg for Flame's life.

☆ CHAPTER TEN ☆

The Fab Four arrived at the slaughterhouse at a quarter to eight.

The first thing they saw was a field with four ponies in and one of them was Flame. He whinnied softly when he saw Flash, and trotted slowly over.

"Oh Flame, Flame! We're here to save you!" creid Flash, stroking his nose.

"Can I help?" said a gruff voice. And the girls turned to see an extremely tall thin man in a flat cap and jodhpurs

"Oh yes! There's been a terrible mistake. This

pony has been sent to be slaughtered, but we want to buy him instead. We've got the money," blurted Flash.

It turned out that the tall man was Mr Gunn, who ran the slaughterhouse. He was a kind man, who liked horses, even though he was in charge of slaughtering them, and he was sympathetic to the girls. It was not the first time he had had someone change their mind at the last minute.

"You're lucky to have got here early," he said. "Come with me, let's see what we can do."

He ushered the girls into a small office and took out some paperwork.

"I can let you have him for £50." said Mr Gunn.

"But I thought it would be £40... I've only got £40," Flash sobbed.

"No, wait," said Lizzy. "We forgot to tell you. Snake gave us £10!"

Flash heaved a huge sigh of relief.

"Mind you, transportation will cost you. And you have got somewhere to keep him, I hope?" Mr Gunn said, more sternly. "There's no point in saving old ponies to lead a miserable half-starved life. I kill 'em, but I kill 'em kindly."

"Yes, yes," said Flash impatiently. "We know all that," and she drew out the sealed envelope of cash that the mayor had given her the night before.

"Right. I'll count it all up, and I think you've got yourselves a deal," said Mr Gunn, opening the envelope. "Oh. I thought you said you had cash?"

The envelope contained, not crisp notes, but crisp gift vouchers for a leading stationer's.

Of course! Whoever heard of a fancy dress party for under-sixteens with a cash prize! Not for

 the first time that week, Flash felt she must be the stupidest person on earth. She broke into heart-rending sobs. She cried so loud and so long that Mr Gunn took pity on her.

"Look, I don't see why we shouldn't accept these," he said. "We need to buy paper, files, order books and all that sort of stuff for our office. So why shouldn't we use vouchers instead of cash?"

And, to the amazement, relief and gratitude of the girls, he agreed to take the vouchers.

Owl immediately rang her father, who had lined up the farmer and a horse box to come and collect Flame if the girls were successful. They stood stroking Flame until the farmer arrived. Flash felt it was the happiest day she had ever spent. But Mr Gunn took the other three ponies off into the yard.

"They'll never come out alive," whispered Owl. "I w-wish we could s-save them all..."

The farmer who came for Flame was a big jolly man. "Now remember," he said to Flash. "I'm taking this pony on condition that you come up and help with him, and the other animals, every Saturday for at least a year. That will be your way of paying for his keep."

Flash agreed, but the others were surprised.

"But Flash," said Lizzy. "That means you won't have time to go up to the stables at weekends."

"Maybe that's a good thing," snorted Flash. "I don't think I want to set eyes on Tom, ever again!"

"But you w-won't be able to r-ride," said Owl.

"Why not?" asked Eclaire, "can't she ride Flame?"

"Certainly not," said the farmer. "This pony's working life is over. That's why he's here," he said, meaningfully, gazing at the closed gate to the yard from which no horse ever emerged alive.

"Look, there are other ponies at the farm – and I want to go and help," said Flash. "It's my only way to pay the farmer back... and I'll learn loads! Won't I?"

"You'll learn a lot about hard work," laughed the farmer kindly. "Now, hop in, I'll give you a lift to the bus."

The girls all piled into the horse box (Owl's father had said this would be OK, since the farmer was an old friend of his) and off they went, gazing sadly back at the empty field and happily back at Flame's two chestnut ears, poking out of the horse box behind them.

☆ CHAPTER ELEVEN ☆

It was a whole week before the Fab Four all got together again. They felt great about saving Flame and also felt that they had been very lucky.

"One of the best things was getting the money from Snake," remembered Lizzy.

"Yeah. It's made me realise he is quite nice and not someone just there cluttering up my space," agreed Flash.

"B-but th-the most amazing thing was your costume," said Owl, admiringly. "H-how did you get time to get back from the stables and dress up?"

At this, Flash roared with laughter.

"I didn't. I fell in the mud and got scratched all over. I spent my bus fare phoning you so I ran all the way to the party. Then I couldn't find you and was suddenly hauled up on stage. I wanted to die! I was much much more suprised than any of you when I won!"

"We've been so lucky," mused Lizzy. "You know, there are lots of slaughterhouses that would never have let us do that."

"Hmmmmm," murmured Flash. "I suppose there's one good thing you could say about Tom, at least he probably knew that he was sending Flame somewhere kind..."

"Oh Flash!" shouted the others all together. "You're not going soft on Tom again are you?"

"Well, I still wouldn't mind looking like Cindy," confessed Flash.

"You must be bonkers" said Lizzy. "You look a trillion times better than that!"

"Y-yes," agreed Owl "Y-you c-can't b-be different from who you are. Anymore than F-Flame could turn into a racehorse..."

"Well, you wanted me to look like a film star," said Flash.

"I did n-not," said Owl, who didn't want the others to know anything about it.

"Anyway, Loretta's look may be great for her, and Cindy's look is fine for her too," said Eclaire, as usual calming everyone down. "But the way you look," Eclaire turned to Flash, enveloping her in a huge hug "is the best of all. Cos..." (and now Owl and Lizzy joined in, while Flash blinked back tears):

"You're YOU.

You're YOU.

You're YOU

that's WHO.

And no one else

In the world will DO!"

"Mind y-you, I'm n-not so s-sure," smiled Owl "I think she looked great as a zombie."

"Er, and you're not still soft on Tom?" asked Lizzy, worried.

"Oh no. I couldn't care less about him," said Flash, adding mysteriously, "I've got Bill to think of now."

"What?" said Owl.

"Eh?" gasped Eclaire.

"WHO'S BILL?!" screamed Lizzy, her worst fears confirmed.

"He's big, with huge dark eyes, rippling muscles and long golden hair. A bit fast, mind you," answered Flash.

"Oh no, Flash. Not again," groaned Lizzy.

"Mmmmm. I'm just off to cook for him," simpered Flash.

"WHAT! COOK for him?" the others cried in horror.

"Yes, a nice bran mash," laughed Flash, "Bill's in the field with Flame and he's got a touch of colic..."